MW01234017

*"Princess Willow & the Magic Fairy Brush"*

**Story Book: 1**

**Written by:** Bundy Renfro
**Edited by:** Bundy Renfro
**Illustrated & Designed by:** Ryan Durney
**Logo Design:** Audrey Durney
**Cover Art:** Ryan Durney

PUBLISHED BY:  4B&B, LLC

ISBN: 978-0-9904545-7-1               Edition: 01

***PrincessWillow.com***

*For my sweet and silly inspirations ~*
*Anna, Kiersten and Jenny...*

*May the memories of brushing your hair be filled with*
*endless fun and magic.*

–Bundy Renfro

# Princess Willow & the Magic Fairy Brush

story by Bundy Renfro

illustrated by Ryan Durney

Deep in an enchanted forest
lives a colony of majestic trees
that walk, talk and play
just like you and me.
Every 100 years,
on the first night of spring
when the full moon shines,
and the tiger lilies sing.

Fairies get together from all across the land
to dust the village with magic seeds, and
soak them deep within the sand.

When the sun awakes, the village fills with anticipation.
Excited trees can't wait to see those new to their habitation.
From the earth the new trees rise—so unique and extraordinary
unlike any seen before, even by Granny Fairy.

News spreads very quickly
led by bunny-riding elves,
but all the creatures of the forest
want to see this for themselves.
To greet the new tree family,
all hurry anxiously.
Never has there sprouted
treefolk of royalty.

"Hello!" salutes the father, "How do you do?
As you can see, my family is anything but few."

They're all very green
and happy, and look
their very best. Except the
youngest daughter, whose
weeping and seems quite stressed.
"This is our youngest—our fussy
little Willow, she always looks as if she
just woke from her pillow. Indeed her
limbs are messy unlike all the rest,
tangled up in knots and filled with
big birds' nests. When we try to keep
her pretty she throws fits, or weeps
and hides. We wish she cared to look as
pretty as we know she is inside."

Listening among the crowd are Mozie Maple and Lucy Spruce.
They shout, "We know just the thing to get those knots and tangles loose.
"Over on the hillside at Salon Flore´ Chateau,
is a famous fairy hairdresser named Francesca Bighairbow."

"Infused into every bristle of her magic brush
is a potion she invented
that causes fairies not to fuss.
Her magic brush works great for fussy fairies,
whose hair is tangled, matted and teased.
She never has to beg to brush their hair,
or ask them pretty please.
And as long as fairies promise
to keep their hair looking nice and neat,
Francesca Bighairbow
gives them a magic brush to keep.
I bet her magic brush will unravel
Willow's tangles wonderfully with ease,
so she can look pretty and feel happy
like the rest of her family of trees."

Little Willow perked up.
She'd been paying close attention,
  wondering about Francesca Bighairbow's
  untangling invention.
She thought..."I don't like throwing fits
  and causing momma so much stress.
I wish to try this magic brush
  Mozie and Lucy kindly suggest."
So, to the crowd she whimpers,
  "I do want to look pretty
and avoid those awkward stares.
Do you think her brush will work for me,
  like it does the fairies' hair?"

With a wink and a grin,
the fairies say,
"Only one way to know!

...'ADIBBIE-DEE-DEE'...

Let's give it a try!"
Then, over little Willow
they all begin to fly.
They run their brushes
through her branches...
what do you think will happen?
Something so amazing,
you just can't imagine.

All the fairies' brushes begin

A kaleidoscope of colors

Beautifully cascading

Willow's branches sway more

to twinkle and glow bright.
fill the moonlit night.
through the glittering sky,
softly than a peaceful lullaby.

Willow has come loose
of her tangles, nests and knots!
She's the most beautiful tree in the forest,
 all the fairies thought.
  Full of joy and excitement
  Willow starts to giggle.
  Her bouncy limbs and leaves
    cause her trunk to dance and wiggle.

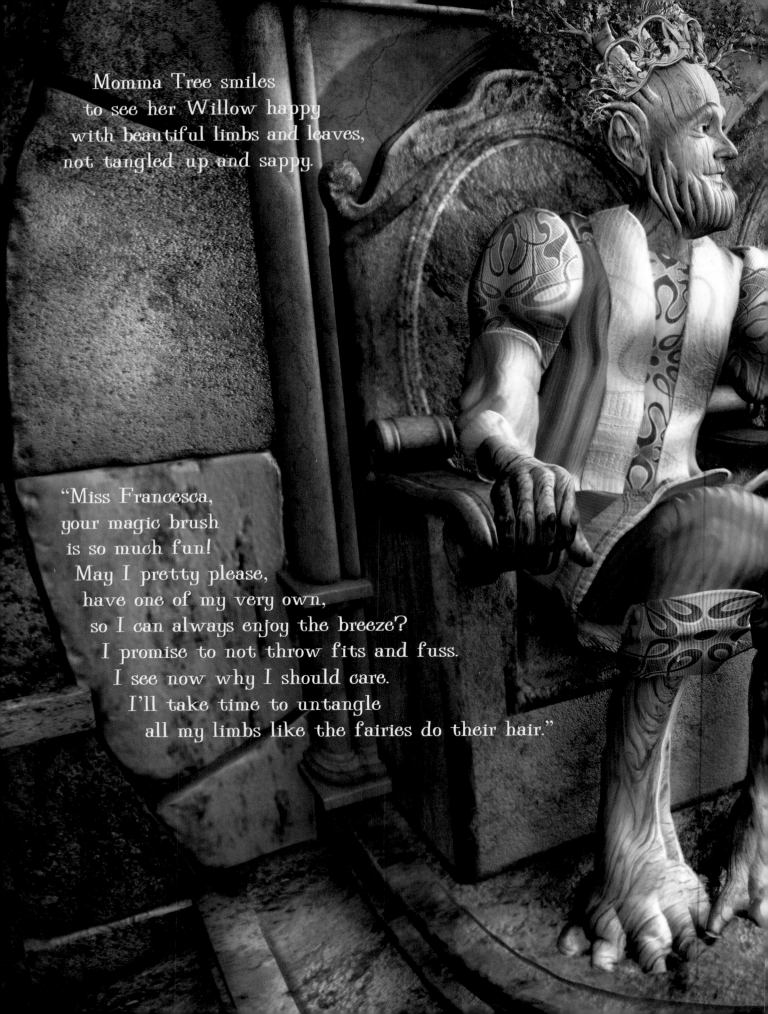

Momma Tree smiles
to see her Willow happy
with beautiful limbs and leaves,
not tangled up and sappy.

"Miss Francesca,
your magic brush
is so much fun!
May I pretty please,
have one of my very own,
so I can always enjoy the breeze?
I promise to not throw fits and fuss.
I see now why I should care.
I'll take time to untangle
all my limbs like the fairies do their hair."

With her magic brush held
high on a ceremonial pillow,
Francesca Bighairbow proudly
says to Princess Willow,
"I'm pleased to present you
with this magic fairy brush
upon which you promise
to use without a fuss."
The trees and fairies cheer,
especially Willow's momma.
No longer will keeping
Willow's hair neat
cause all those
tears and drama!

From the magic brush she earns,
a valuable lesson Willow learns.
No matter rain or shine,
to feel pretty all the time,
every girl must start
with a pure and lovely heart.

So good or bad hair day
she's beautiful in every way!

the end

P

Bundy Renfro, a graduate of The University of Texas at Austin, earned a bachelor's degree in Advertising with a minor in Educational Psychology.

Bundy has always had a love for poetry and creative writing. She loves writing

PrincessWillow.com / @BundyRenfro

uplifting stories that help children and adults solve problems, face challenges and build character. Inspired by her faith and moved by life's trials, Bundy knows we can all use help no matter how big or small the challenge.

When asked to write a story encouraging girls to brush their hair, Bundy couldn't wait to deliver a poetic story uniquely imaginative and girly! With no girls of her own, Bundy thought back to her childhood. She remembered the dreaded tangles, mandatory brushing and blow drying, sleeping in sponge rollers and who could forget those TEXAS size big hair bows! It all came back to her, and before she knew it the world of Princess Willow was flowing from her more freely than glitter flows from the hands of little children. It didn't take her long to realize this small favor would take on bigger proportions. Bundy is pleased to present *Princess Willow & the Magic Fairy Brush,* the first book in the Princess Willow series. She hopes this magical fairytale brings you joyful memories to be cherished for many years to come.

For all her hard work, Francesca Bighairbow awarded Bundy her very own Magic Fairy Brush. Francesca can't wait for you to experience her magic brush for yourself. Like Princess Willow and Bundy, we can all use a little magic in our lives!

When not frequenting a land of butterflies and bunnies, Bundy lives in Texas with her husband, Dusty and their two sons Knox and Nash.

Ryan Durney is an award-winning, full-time freelance illustrator who most often works on children's books, fantasy, science fiction and prehistoric creatures.

Ryan has a life-long obsession with fairy tales, mythology and antiquated ephemera. He enjoys bringing strange, difficult subjects to gasping life on the page or screen.

He has won several awards for his work, including many international competitions such as *Best of Fantasy,* placement in *Society of Illustrators West #45,* and a *Mom's Choice Award* in 2012 and 2011. His favorite recognition was being voted in by the kids for a *Children's Choice Award* in 2008.

Ryan has recently written and illustrated a book of bird mythology, *Birds of Lore.* He works in his studio in Austin, alongside his wife, Audrey Durney—also a talented artist and his greying pug, Royal Allen Durney.

RyanDurney.com / @Unknown_Tome
Hire An Illustrator: http://illo.cc/44158

# CERTIFICATE
## OF AWARD

For your promise to not throw fits and fuss and to care to brush your hair, Francesca Bighairbow proudly awards you, _____,

on this _____ day of _____ 20____

your very own Magic Fairy Brush.  May the memories of brushing your hair be filled with endless fun and magic!

Love Always,

*Francesca Bighairbow*